Meghan Rose

IS Out of THiS world

written by
Lori Z. Scott

illustrated by
Stacy Curtis

Standard®
PUBLISHING

Cincinnati, Ohio

Published by Standard Publishing, Cincinnati, Ohio
www.standardpub.com

Text Copyright © 2011 by Lori Z. Scott
Illustrations Copyright © 2011 by Stacy Curtis

Printed in: USA
Project editor: Diane Stortz

ISBN 978-0-7847-2932-8

Library of Congress Cataloging-in-Publication Data

Scott, Lori Z., 1965-
  Meghan Rose is out of this world / written by Lori Z. Scott ; illustrated by Stacy Curtis.
     p. cm.
  Summary: Meghan Rose is afraid that her friends will be so impressed by Sophie's jump-rope skills that they will not want to play with Meghan anymore, so she tells a lie to reclaim their attention.
  ISBN 978-0-7847-2932-8
 [1. Honesty--Fiction. 2. Christian life--Fiction. 3. Friendship--Fiction. 4. Schools--Fiction.] I. Curtis, Stacy, ill. II. Title.
  PZ7.S42675Mc 2011
  [Fic]--dc22
                                    2010040176

17 16 15 14 13 12 11   9 8 7 6 5 4 3 2 1

Contents

Dogs and Ducks and Gravity

"Hey, everyone! Thank you for coming to my show! Now I, Meghan Rose Thompson, first-grade superstar, will jump rope and recite a new chant I made up called 'Dogs, They Sure Can Bark and Drool.'"

I bowed to my friends Lynette, Ryan, and Adam. They watched from the top of the monkey bars with their feet dangling down.

My friend Kayla was hanging upside

down on a low bar with her back to me. Her two blond piggy tails dangled like tiny worms on a fish hook, only without the slime.

"Who's talking?" Kayla said.

I stepped up and tapped her shoulder. "Me. I'm right here."

Kayla grabbed the bar and swung down. "Good. I have a new chant too. It's called 'Ducks, They Sure Are Cute and Yellow and Fluffy and Quacky-Wacky. And So Are Snorkels.'"

Lynette jumped off the bars and landed next to Kayla with a *WUMP*. She smoothed down her pink shirt and straightened her huge hair bow.

You wouldn't catch me wearing one of those things. Nothing but gravity holds my hair in place.

By the way, gravity is not the brown stuff you put on mashed potatoes to make them tasty. That's *gravy*. Gravity is what keeps the gravy from floating off your mashed potatoes and the mashed potatoes from floating off your plate and your plate from floating off the table.

I'm gravy smart because of my Grandma Wright's cooking.

I'm gravity smart because of my first-grade teacher, Mrs. Arnold. Last week I jumped off the reading couch during indoor recess. I thought it would shoot me toward outer space, like the cow jumping over the moon. But it didn't. I landed KER-SMASH on the floor instead. Mrs. Arnold gave me a quick science lesson.

She's that kind of teacher.

She said gravity is an unseen force

that pulls things—like kids jumping off a couch—toward the ground. Gravity gives things weight.

I also learned I should watch what I say about gravity. When I told Mrs. Arnold she looked like she put on some extra gravity, she sent me to the thinking chair.

Anyway, Lynette said, "*Quacky-wacky* isn't a word. And snorkels aren't anything like ducks."

"Blah, blah, blah," said Kayla. "Can I do my chant or not?"

"Sure," I said. "Right after me."

I got a beat going with the jump rope. *Thump. Thump. Thump. Thump.* Then I chanted,

"The dogs next door bark oh so sweet,
And they dance all day
To a doggie-woggie beat.

But that's not all those dogs can do—
Those furry friends can also drool!
With an arf, arf, woof
And a slicky-licky too,
The dogs next door sure bark and drool!"
Everyone clapped.

"Ta-da!" I said. "Your turn, Kayla."

"Yay! Thank you!" Kayla said. She turned the jump rope. *Thump. Thump. Thump. Thump.* She chanted,

"Duck, duck, snorkel, snorkel,
Duck, duck, duck!
Duck, duck, snorkel, snorkel,
Duck, duck, duck!
Duck, duck—"

"What is it with you and ducks?"

I knew that voice. It belonged to Sophie, from Mrs. Killeen's class across the hall. Her friend Carly was with her.

Sophie and I don't always get along. Maybe because Sophie likes to win and I always seem to beat her. Still, I hoped that someday we could get along the way we did when we played Duck, Duck, Goose at recess with all our friends and had a blast.

"Sophie! Carly!" I said. "Do you want to jump rope with us?"

Carly looked at Sophie. Sophie looked at me. I felt like a show dog standing in front of the judges. Without meaning to, I stood up taller.

"I guess so," Sophie said. "But only if I can jump RIGHT NOW and by myself."

"Use my jump rope," I said, holding it out.

Sophie took it. "Watch this."

"Thanks," I blurted.

"I didn't start yet," Sophie said.

"I know. But my mom always says it's polite to thank people when they do something nice for you."

"Well, you're not my mother," Sophie snapped. "Now watch this." She glanced at Carly and then zippy-quick started jumping.

She jumped on one foot. The other foot. Then red-hot pepper. Then crisscross. Then backward.

My friends watched her with their eyes going back and forth like big tire swings.

Lynette gasped.

Ryan and Adam punched the air and cheered, "GO, GO, GO!"

Plus Kayla's mouth fell open far enough to show that thing that hangs in the back of your throat that looks like a tiny red balloon except it's upside down and slimy.

Sophie was that good.

My heart went *BUMP-bump*. Maybe Sophie was *too* good at jumping rope. Maybe she was so good, my friends would like Sophie better than me. Maybe—POOF— they'd leave me so they could play with her.

Nah. What a silly idea.

Then Lynette said, "Sophie, I never knew you were so *amazing!*"

This time my heart beat *BUMP-BUMP*.

Silly idea? Maybe not.

I Don't Believe It

"Sophie, you jump faster than a blink," Ryan said. "And I don't know anyone else who can do crisscross like that."

"Sophie!" Kayla squealed. "You might be the best jump roper EVER."

Sophie gave us a don't-I-know-it kind of smile. "Yes, I probably am," she said.

I thought *I* was the best jump roper ever. And the best friend ever.

"You mean, 'Thank you, yes, I probably

am,'" I said with a flat voice. "My mom says—"

Sophie made a huffy noise.

I huffed right back. "I was just trying to be helpful."

"What else can you do, Sophie?" Kayla asked.

"Probably nothing," I said quickly.

But Sophie shrugged and scrambled up the monkey bars. Balancing on the top, she slowly stood with her arms straight out. She held that pose for a few seconds and then swung down.

"WOWIE!" Kayla said.

"Yeah," Sophie said, straightening out her shirt in a la-de-da way. "I learned that tricky move last summer from a famous dance instructor, Mrs. Rolls."

"Does she have a son named Brock

Nelson?" I asked. "You know . . . Brock N. Rolls?"

Sophie gave me a stop-interrupting look. "Mrs. Rolls said I had the kind of balance and charm needed to star in a high-wire act. I got to wear the most flashy, glittery red dress in the show."

"You were in the circus?" Kayla gasped.

"I don't believe it!" I said.

It couldn't be true! But if it was . . . then for sure all my friends would want to play with Sophie instead of me.

Sophie swung her head so everyone could see the glittery red headband in her hair. "Yes. Where do you think this headband came from?" she said.

"I'm sure . . . it came from . . . the In a Pickle Store," I stammered. "They sell all kinds of shiny stuff for hair. Plus shiny stuff for skin. And shiny stuff for toenails. And maybe even shiny stuff for armpits. It couldn't be from a *real* circus."

I couldn't imagine Sophie's mother letting her do something as risky as a high-wire circus act. At least not without letting the whole school know first. And bringing a reporter to interview Sophie for the news. And selling book and movie rights.

Sophie frowned at me. "It was a summer dance camp with a circus theme. We performed a program called 'Under the Big Top.' I had the starring role—the high-wire dancer."

"WOWIE!" Kayla said. "That's cooler than a closet full of ducks!"

"Can I have your autograph?" Ryan said.

"Me too?" Adam added.

Lynette sighed and gave Sophie a dreamy look. "I wish *I* had a glittery headband like that."

Somehow the big looks my friends gave Sophie made me feel small. Which made me want to do something EXTRA EXCITING to remind them what a good, fun, wonderful, better-than-Sophie friend I am.

I just didn't know what that extra-exciting something was.

The recess whistle blew, and everyone made a mad dash to line up.

That's because being first in line means getting to the drinking fountain first.

And that's important because who likes waiting? I can only wait for a minute and fourteen seconds before I get the wiggles.

And everyone knows you're supposed to leave wiggles outside on the playground . . .

along with feelings of being smaller and less important than Sophie.

Too bad I never was very good at leaving my wiggles—or anything else—behind.

To Tell the Truth (Sort Of)

After recess it was time for science. Mrs. Arnold turned out the lights in our room. Mrs. Arnold is full of surprises. Either that or she needed a nap. It *was* Monday, after all.

At first, we jabbered away. What was Mrs. Arnold up to now? Then the noise dropped to whispers. Something about darkness makes that happen.

Mrs. Arnold said softly, "If you look at the night sky, you'll see stars."

She flicked a switch, and a ball with tiny holes in it lit up.

"Look up at the ceiling," she said.

We did.

We gasped. The ceiling of our classroom
looked like a sky full of glowing stars.

"It's like someone sliced off the roof at night," Lynette whispered.

I was too dazzled to say anything.

Mrs. Arnold continued in a hushed voice. "Long ago, when people looked up at the night sky and saw stars, some picked out patterns of stars that seemed to form pictures." She pointed to a section of the ceiling with a yardstick. "For example, this group of stars looks like a soup spoon or a ladle. It's a constellation commonly known as the Big Dipper. We'll learn more about stars and planets these next few weeks as we study outer space."

Kids around the room made *ooh* and *ahh* sounds. What could be more exciting than studying space?

Maybe learning where earwax comes from. Or what happens when you swallow a bug. Or why gravy is always white or brown but never purple. I've wondered about those things.

Mrs. Arnold turned the lights back on. "Can anyone share something you already know about space?"

Lynette's arm shot into the air like a rocket. "The sun is the star closest to Earth, and Mars is the closest planet."

Mrs. Arnold nodded. "Very good."

Kayla bounced in her seat, hand in the air. "The moon is made of cheese," she said.

"It looks like it," Mrs. Arnold said. "But the moon is not made of cheese."

"Oh," Kayla said. "Then is it a cookie?"

I thought that was a good question. After all, Mars and the Milky Way are candy bars.

"No," Mrs. Arnold said, "but we'll keep

your ideas in mind as we learn."

"Neil Armstrong was the first person to walk on the moon," Ryan said.

"And a cow jumped over it," Adam added.

That gave me an idea. "Oh!" I said, waving my hand. "Oh, oh, oh!"

"Meghan?"

"You said gravity pulls things and gives things weight. So I bet gravity also holds the moon close to Earth."

Mrs. Arnold smiled. "That's right. Now you're thinking like a scientist."

I saw Lynette and Kayla look at me with WOWIE in their eyes. Folding my hands on my desk, I sat up straight and tall. I felt powerful and important, like a school bus driver.

"Thank you, Mrs. Arnold," I said. And

then for some reason—maybe because Sophie was on my mind—my mouth kept talking. "I went to Junior Astronaut Space Camp last summer," I said.

The class gasped.

And I knew right then: SPACE CAMP was the extra-exciting something I needed! It would WOW my friends so much, they wouldn't think twice about Sophie. Maybe space camp would wow Sophie too, enough to make her want to be my friend.

"I even ate space food like an astronaut," I said. "A dried-up ice cream sandwich!"

That got more *oohs* and *ahhs*. I gave everyone—especially my friends—my biggest movie-star smile.

Mrs. Arnold smiled too. "A stellar comment, Meghan. One of the things we'll learn about is how an astronaut's diet is similar to ours as well as different. We'll even try astronaut ice cream. I think it will taste out of this world!"

"Is 'out of this world' alien talk for 'Take me to your leader, earthling'?" Kayla asked.

"It means 'fantastic,'" Mrs. Arnold said.

"In that case," Kayla said, "Meghan Rose is out of this world, because she went to space camp!"

Some of the kids cheered.

It was *soooo* perfect! Now I had only one small problem.

I actually *didn't* go to Junior Astronaut Space Camp last summer.

I wanted to go, but Mom said no. Apparently you have to be at least eight years old to be spacey enough for camp.

But my cousin David went, and he told

me about it and brought me some astronaut food.

I also checked out three library books about space to look at the pictures.

And I have a telescope.

Plus last year I visited a planetarium show at a science museum.

So putting all those space experiences together was kind of, sort of, almost, nearly, more or less close enough to actually going to space camp. And the itty-bitty, teensy-weensy fact that I didn't truly go wasn't really a lie.

Right?

The WOWIE Factor

At lunch the next day, Kayla plopped down her tray next to mine. "I can't wait for science today," she said.

"Me neither," Lynette said. "I hope we start with the moon. Did you know there is no air on the moon?"

"Did you also know the moon has lower gravity than Earth?" I said. "I'd weigh less on the moon. If I jumped rope there, I'd jump six times higher!"

"Just think what Sophie could do with a jump rope on the moon," Kayla said. "She'd jump all the way to Mars! We should tell her about it."

Sophie again. I frowned. "Sophie would need to learn about space first," I said. "Like I did at space camp."

Kayla's eyes got big. "I forgot about that!" she said.

I knew I had her attention. Questions started shooting out of her mouth like firecrackers. "Did you ride in a rocket?"

"No. But I saw one."

That was the truth. I saw a picture of a rocket in a book.

"Did you wear a helmet?"

"Yes." I didn't mention that it was a motorcycle helmet, and I was at my cousin David's house at the time.

"How about a space suit?"

"Yes." Pajamas had to count because of all the extra space in them.

"Do space suits have zippers? What if you get all suited up and then have to use the restroom? And how do toilets work without gravity, anyway?"

I quick took a bite of my sandwich so I wouldn't have to answer.

It didn't matter. Kayla didn't pause. "And what kind of space food did you eat?"

"Yeah," Ryan said, sitting down across from me. "Did they serve launch? Get it? Lunch . . . launch?"

Adam squeezed in beside Ryan. "Did you play with any of the equipment? What about toys? Do yo-yos work in space?"

I swallowed. My food went down like a big lump of mashed potatoes without gravy.

"I, um . . ."

"Please, people, get it right," Lynette said. She sounded annoyed. "Meghan wasn't in space."

A wave of *uh-oh* hit me. I held my breath, waiting to see what she'd say next.

"Meghan went to space *camp*," Lynette said. "Yo-yos work at space camp because there is still gravity."

"Oh," Adam said.

Relieved, I let out my air with a hiss.

I took another bite of my sandwich and thought hard about the camp pictures I had seen. What else did I know about space that would impress my friends and keep them wanting to play with me and not Sophie?

Lynette interrupted my thinking. "What I want to know is why you never mentioned space camp before yesterday."

For the second time, a wave of *uh-oh* shot through me. I fumbled with my milk carton. "I didn't think it was any big deal," I said, trying to use a la-de-da voice like Sophie.

"Are you nuts?" Ryan said, slapping his forehead. "You went to SPACE CAMP! That is so out of this world!"

"Tell us more," Kayla said.

Shaking my head, I bit my lip.

"Please?" Kayla begged.

"Did you learn anything about the moon?" Lynette asked.

"Did you get to use those radio walkie-talkies?" Ryan said.

"I bet you saw astro-ducks!" Kayla said.

"Tell us!" Adam said.

"Please, please, please, please!" seemed to burst from everyone at once.

So I told about countdowns and comets

and capsules. I told about lasers and liftoffs and light years. I told about moonbeams and sunbeams and balance beams.

I couldn't stop. One thing led to another.

My friends seemed to drink it all up.

And it was all TRUE, TRUE, TRUE! But my friends didn't know I learned it from a book and a Saturday-morning cartoon, not from space camp.

We spent our whole lunch recess playing astronauts.

"Meghan, you can be captain," Ryan said. "Because you went to space camp."

Using the monkey bars as our spaceship, we battled aliens and blasted meteors out of the sky. We lay across the top bars with our arms straight out and pretended we were floating.

I kept hoping Sophie would walk by and

see how my friends felt about me. Maybe she'd hear about space camp and think I was WOWIE too. But she never came by.

The recess whistle blew right when we landed on a new planet.

"Rats!" Ryan said. "Let's finish this tomorrow!"

Super Cats and Not-So-Super Acts

The next day on the playground, Ryan called, "Captain, I think I've spotted a new alien life-form in the grass."

I turned to my shipmates. "We'd better check it out. Lieutenant Lynette, Cadet Kayla, come with me. Adam, three to send down."

Adam frowned. "What about me?"

"You're the doctor. You have to stay here

in case we need help."

"I have a hangnail," Kayla said. She held out her finger.

"Never mind," I snapped. "You'll live. Now Adam, send us down!"

Adam saluted and then gave Lynette, Kayla, and me each a small push on the shoulder. One by one we dropped out of the monkey bars and landed on the ground.

I clicked on my pretend wrist speaker. "Thank you, Adam," I said.

"What?" Ryan said. "No one says thank-you in space movies."

"But my mom always says it's polite to say thank-you when someone does something nice for you."

"It just doesn't seem very captainlike," Ryan said.

Kayla took a step forward, but I threw

out my hand to stop her. "Wait! We don't know what we're getting into. This could be dangerous. Better pull out your nonviolent, childproof, nontoxic, parent-and-teacher-approved weapons!"

Everyone just stared at me.

"That means pick weapons that no one will tattle on us about," I explained.

I plucked a long blade of grass and waved it in front of me like a sword.

Kayla nodded. "Gotcha."

Lynette crouched and held her hands in a karate position.

Kayla pulled a rubber ducky out of her pocket and gave it a strong squeeze.

"A rubber ducky?" I said.

"You never know when one of these will come in handy," Kayla said. "And this ducky has a mean squeak."

I glanced at Lynette and sighed. "At least you know karate," I whispered.

"Not really," Lynette whispered back. "But I know a lot of big words, and I'm not afraid to use them. Like this."

She yelled, "SESQUIPEDALIAN!" and chopped the air. Then she straightened her hair bow. "That means 'the use of big words.'"

"Very scary," I said.

"Hurry up!" Ryan called. "Our alien life-form is crawling away!"

We all rushed over, including Adam, who jumped ship without orders.

"It's a WORM!" Kayla squealed.

"It's a caterpillar," Lynette corrected.

"IT'S SUPER CAT!" I yelled.

Kayla scrunched up her face.

Lynette squinted at me.

Jokes are no fun when you have to explain them.

"Super Cat," I said. "It's super, and the cat part is short for *caterpillar*."

Ryan gasped. "You can call it Super Caterpillar if you want, but never, never, never mess with the name of the *real* Super Cat hero. That's just *wrong*."

He picked up Super Caterpillar and held it.

Some kids ran over to see what was going on. Carly came too.

Then Sophie showed up. And it was a what-could-be-more-exciting-than-me kind of showed up.

All the kids were *oohing* and *ahhing* and asking, "Can I hold it?"

Kayla leaned close to me. "Is now a good time for the rubber-ducky attack?"

"No."

Kayla didn't listen. She held up the duck and gave it a big squeeze.

"Back off, people!" Kayla said. "We found this creature in outer space . . . and it needs . . . SPACE!"

"You did not find it in outer space," Sophie said.

She didn't have the WOWIE look on her face that I wanted to see. Hmm . . .

"You're right, Sophie," I said. "We found the caterpillar right here. It's just a plain old ordinary bug. We pretended we landed on another planet and found it. And I am leading the mission because last summer I went to . . . *space camp*."

Sophie's mouth and eyes looked like big letter *O*s.

Then Carly said, "Wow, Meghan! I've

never met anyone who went to space camp."

Then POOF, the *ooh-ahh* look fell off Sophie's face. She frowned and folded her arms. "Anyone can go to space camp," she said.

"But not anyone here did but me," I said.

"Really?" she said. "Can you prove it?"

Her words hung in the air like yesterday's laundry on a clothesline.

"Of course Meghan can prove it," Lynette said. "Why would she lie?"

My tummy flip-flopped. Lynette's words were like a paper cut—it stings right away but doesn't start bleeding until you check it.

The sting—*OW!* How could I prove a lie? And the blood—*OH NO!* How could I tell the whole truth now?

Rocket Scientist

Frozen like a pepperoni pizza, I stared at Lynette with my mouth open. She ignored me.

"Maybe you can show us something you'd find only at space camp," Lynette suggested. "Like astronaut toothpaste. That would prove it."

"Or I could show you a camp flyer," I said, thinking fast.

"Or a space camp T-shirt," Lynette

continued. "Campers always get those."

"Or a camp flyer," I repeated.

"No," Sophie said. "That's too easy. How about . . . ." She tapped her chin. The WOWIE look crept back into her eyes. "Could you show us how a rocket works?"

"Of course," I said.

All the kids cheered.

Then before you could say what-do-you-mean-you-can-show-us-how-a-rocket-works-are-you-crazy, the whistle blew. One *TWEET* and my fate was sealed.

Tomorrow I would show everyone how a rocket works.

Just like I learned at space camp.

GULP!

You don't have to be a rocket scientist to figure out I was in trouble.

I followed the other kids to line up, but

my legs moved like melted cheese. At times like this, I'm glad I have two ears but only one mouth. I always seem to get trouble out of my mouth. And so far, I've only gotten wax out of my ears.

I wished lies didn't give you the I'm-so-amazing-you-can't-help-but-love-me feeling AND the *uh-oh*-someone-is-going-to-catch-me-lying-and-realize-I'm-not-so-amazing-after-all feeling.

What was I going to do?

Besides end up last in line for the drinking fountain.

At the end of the day, while I loaded up my backpack, Ryan joked, "Tomorrow will be a blast. Get it?"

"Ha, ha, ha," I said.

Ryan kept going. "When you show your

rocket, I bet you'll need a lot of space."

"Ha, ha," I said.

"If your shoes come untied tomorrow, I'll teach you how to tie an ASTRO-knot."

"Ha," I said, lifting my backpack.

"I'll count down the hours until next *launch* recess."

"Sorry. I don't have a single *ha* left. All gone. And so am I."

I took off for the bus line.

"Wait!" Ryan said. "Don't you want to hear more jokes?"

Sighing, I stopped to wait for him.

Because that's what friends do. Wait.

Even when they know waiting might mean hearing another bad space joke.

"Thanks," Ryan said.

"I'm glad you said that. My mom always says—"

"I know, I know. 'It's polite to say thank-you when someone does something nice for you.' Now, what do you get when you cross a spaceship with a banana? A rocket-slip!"

I didn't laugh. I didn't chuckle, tee-hee, giggle, or smile. I didn't even groan. I just kept walking.

Ryan frowned. "Don't you get it?"

"Of course," I snapped.

"Then why are you so grumpy?" Ryan asked. "Aren't you excited about showing us how a rocket works tomorrow?"

"That's the problem! I don't know how to do that. I don't know anything about—" AHHH! I snapped my mouth shut. Hard. Because without meaning to, I had almost let the truth slip out!

Ryan didn't seem to notice. "Right," he said, nodding. "I get it. At space camp, they

45

probably showed you how a rocket works using a *real rocket*. And of course there are no real rockets on the playground. That is a problem."

"R-r-right. That's it."

"Hmm," Ryan said. "Now I see the gravity of your situation."

I made a huffy sound.

"OK, no more jokes," he said. "What you need is something to spark your brain."

He fished around in his backpack. "Maybe this will help." He handed me something rubbery and blue.

"It's a flat balloon," I said.

"It's *blue*. Your favorite color."

Stretching it like a rubber band, I aimed it at him. "It's flat. It has a hole."

"But your brain is doing some figuring out now, right?"

"I figured out it's flat," I said. Then I let go. *SNAP!* The balloon hit Ryan *SMACK* on the shoulder.

"Yay!" Ryan cheered. "You snapped out of it."

I couldn't help it. I giggled.

So did Ryan.

We giggled all the way to the bus. Because that's something else friends do. Giggle. Even if they know giggling might lead to another bad joke.

I picked up the balloon and stuck it in my pocket.

"So you like it?" Ryan asked.

"No. It's flat."

For some reason that made us giggle even more.

But it didn't help me figure out how a rocket works.

The Gravity of the Situation

After I got off the bus, I went straight to my room and sat on my bed.

I wanted to think and figure stuff out.

First I thought, *What am I going to do?*

Then I figured out that I didn't know.

Should I tell the truth? That idea made my stomach hurt. What would my friends think of me? What would Sophie think?

I *had* to keep pretending going to space

camp was true.

Of course, the idea of having to keep lying made my stomach hurt too. But I ignored it.

Instead I picked up a space book. Maybe I could find an idea there.

My mom told me once that she prays before reading her Bible and asks God to help her understand the words better. Even though this was a space book, I decided maybe I should pray too. Because I needed all the help I could get.

I squeezed my eyes shut. "Hello, God," I said. "I've got a problem. I told a teensy-weensy little story about something. Now I'm trying to figure out what to do. No one got hurt. But I don't want to get caught."

My prayer was not coming out right. I needed help with a rocket. I didn't want to deal with the whole close-enough-to-be-the-truth-but-not-really thing. In fact, I didn't want to think about it, not even if it were a pile of potatoes covered in purple gravy.

After all, I knew better. I knew God wanted me to tell the truth. I learned that the day I decided to throw Dad's comb into the toilet.

Don't blame me too much. I'm a curious girl. And I wanted to see if his comb floated. It did. Even when I flushed.

But then my dad walked in.

He saw his floating comb and then he saw me. "Meghan Rose!" he bellowed. "Did you put my comb in the toilet?"

"No," I lied. "I didn't even touch it. I believe the comb got hot and decided to go for a swim all on its own."

He frowned at me.

"Whew," I said, fanning my face. "It's

burning hot in here. I don't blame your comb for jumping in the toilet like that."

"Really?" Dad put his hands on my shoulders. "Listen to me, Meghan Rose. The Bible tells us that the way we live matters to God. We need to tell the truth, even when it's hard to do."

So I told the truth. And Dad was right. It was hard to do.

Then I had to fish the comb out of the toilet.

Still, even though I remembered that cold toilet water, there was NO WAY I was going to admit to my friends that I lied.

Maybe admitting I lied wasn't the best way to start my prayer.

Or maybe it was.

I took a big breath and tried again. "God, I'm sorry I lied. And I promise I'll try to always tell the truth as soon as this whole thing is over. But right now, I need help showing how a rocket works. So I'm asking for a good plan. Amen."

Somehow I still felt like I had just thrown Dad's comb into the toilet, but I reminded myself I'd be honest . . . next time.

For now, I went back to my book and started looking for ideas. After flipping though what seemed like a million pictures of different planets, stars, and moons, I finally found some of a rocket.

And guess what? The book explained how rockets work!

Blast Off

I didn't understand all the words in the book, but I learned a few things from the pictures.

A rocket has a bunch of fuel on the inside. When something lights that stuff up, it makes gas.

The gas must need more space than what is inside the rocket, because arrows in one picture showed gas escaping out the back. And that's what pushes the rocket forward!

I laughed for ten whole minutes when I figured all that out. Because I KNOW how gas works after one of my mom's chili dinners. One bowl and my belly gets full of gas . . . and escapes out my backside. I call them toots.

Then BLAM! I got an idea! Maybe I could explain how rockets work with a bowl of my mom's chili!

But then I tried to imagine how my friends would react. I decided that idea stunk.

How would I actually build a rocket, anyway?

I thought harder.

If I cut out a large square from a plastic grocery bag and taped sticks on two sides and looped a string between them and added a tail, I could make a kite. With a black marker I could draw a rocket and make it a rocket kite. Of course, the whole fuel idea would be lost. Plus everyone would say, "That's just a kite."

Right.

An empty roll of toilet paper might work for a rocket, but it wouldn't hold fuel.

An empty water bottle has a rocket kind of shape and would hold fuel . . . but what would I use for fuel?

Soda pop! If I took a bottle of soda pop and shook, shook, shook it up, pop would explode—*PFOOM*—out the top! After that, I could explain how that pop was like rocket fuel. Perfect!

Except I was pretty sure Mrs. Arnold wouldn't enjoy that messy little show.

I needed something else that would work without making a mess. Maybe I could take a water-bottle cap and shoot it with a rubber band. Or not. The cap might work as a rocket, but as far as fuel goes, using a rubber band would be a real stretch.

Rubber band! A real stretch! Ha! That was the kind of joke Ryan would like!

Thinking about Ryan reminded me about my flat blue balloon.

And BLAM! Just like that, an idea flew into my head! A BALLOON rocket! With air for fuel!

I jumped off my bed and raced down the stairs. In Mom's party stash I found a sack of balloons and pulled out a blue one.

I puffed and puffed and puffed and puffed until the balloon looked big and round and my head felt dizzy.

Then I practiced my speech. "Let me show you how a rocket works. When I blew up my balloon rocket, I filled it with fuel.

When I let go, the fuel will shoot out the back, and the rocket will go forward."

I let go. The balloon zipped around the room in crazy circles, going *pppffffttt! pppffffttt! pppffffttt!* until the air ran out and the balloon fell *SPLAT* on the floor.

Then I zipped around the room in crazy circles yelling, "Whoopee! WOWIE! *Wheeeeeee!*"

My balloon rocket wasn't perfect—I don't know anything that flies in such a wild way—but it worked.

And when Kayla and Lynette and Ryan and Adam saw it, I bet they'd say, "Wow, Meghan, you're amazing. You're the best friend in the world." And they'd forget all about Sophie.

Plus no one would ever guess I'd never been to space camp!

I clapped and clapped for myself.

Tomorrow might turn out to be a real gas after all!

Even without Mom's chili.

Countdown

At lunch the next day, I felt like freshly popped popcorn. Full of *ZING* and *ZANG* and *POP* (but without that yummy touch of butter).

I wasn't the only one excited about the day. Kayla plopped down next to me at the table and begged, "Please, please, please tell me what you're going to do."

I grinned. "You'll just have to wait and see."

She didn't give up. "Please?"

"Nope."

"I'll sing you a song if you tell me."

"Nope."

"I'll do a duck dance if you tell me."

"Is it like a chicken dance?"

"Yes."

"In that case, nope."

"I'll give you my straw if you tell me."

I held up my chocolate milk. "I already have a straw. You'll just have to wait."

I took a long drink through my straw. And BLAM! Just like that, I knew how to fix my balloon's wild-flying problem.

By adding a straw, yarn, and tape to my balloon rocket, I could win not only a two-thumbs-up review from my friends but from Sophie too!

I spotted Sophie across the lunchroom.

Her skirt glittered like ant-sized camera flashes. I just hoped her WOWIE look didn't out-WOWIE my rocket trick and steal all my friends' attention again.

With a nervous sigh, I glanced at the clock. I had just enough time before recess started to get the lunch ladies' permission to collect my supplies from Mrs. Arnold's craft box.

My pockets puffed out like marshmallows when I joined my friends and Sophie and Carly by the monkey bars. I handed Sophie the end of a long piece of yarn. "Would you please stand here and hold this?"

Sophie took the yarn. I said, "Thank you. My mom always says it's polite to say thank-you when someone does something nice for you."

Sophie frowned, so I quickly added, "But

you knew that. Already. OK. So. Now . . .
stay right there." I pulled the yarn long and
straight. Then I slipped the straw on the end.
The straw fit like a train on a track.

After that, I handed the other end of the
yarn to Kayla and started blowing up my
balloon.

"What do I do?" Kayla asked.

I stopped blowing up the balloon and
squeezed the end shut. "Just stand there," I
said.

"That's all?" Kayla said. "I can stand
more than that."

"I bet you can. You could stand in line,
stand out in the rain, and stand by me," I
said. "But right now, just stand there."

When the balloon looked full, I held it
up. "I promised to show you all how a rocket
works," I said. "Since I couldn't build one,

this balloon will be my rocket."

"Why didn't you tie it off?" Kayla asked.

"Because the air inside the balloon acts like fuel in a rocket. When rocket fuel burns, it makes gas. That gas has to go somewhere . . . and the only place to go is OUT. Gas shooting out pushes the rocket forward— just like air coming out of the balloon.

"To keep the balloon going straight instead of wild all over the place, I'm going to tape it to this straw, and then I'll send it down the line of yarn."

I held the end of the balloon tightly, making sure it faced Kayla. Lynette helped me tape the balloon to the straw.

When all was ready, I said, "Help me count down."

Everyone joined in. "Five! Four! Three!

Two! One! Blast off!"

I let go. The balloon zipped *pppfffttt!* right toward Sophie.

"*Whoa!*" the kids said.

"TA-DA!" I said. "And THAT'S how a rocket works!"

After that, all the kids, even Sophie, wanted to try it. And so they did, one after another.

Pppfffttt! "Ooh!"

Pppfffttt! "Ahh!"

Pppfffttt! "Whoa!"

When the recess whistle blew, I walked with bouncy steps to line up with Sophie and Carly.

"I love that trick!" Sophie said. "I'm going to show my mom when I get home."

"Sure," I said. "It's fun to do."

"Space camp sounds like fun."

I nodded. "You should try it sometime."

"Good idea," Sophie said. "I'll ask my mom to call your mom after school. Then your mom can give my mom all the details about the camp."

I stopped bouncing. "Details?"

"Yes. You know . . . where it's at. How much it costs. How long it takes to drive there. Whether or not parents get to visit or call while you are there. Do you need to

bring extra money? That kind of stuff."

I. Stopped. Right. There.

My tummy did a flip. Plus I felt dizzy.

If Sophie's mom called my mom, Sophie would know I lied. Even worse, my friends would find out I lied. How could I face them? They'd have even more reason to leave *me* to be *Sophie's* friends instead.

Plus my mom and dad wouldn't be too happy, either.

"Are you OK?" Sophie asked.

"Yes." I swallowed and gave her a weak smile. "I'm just a little spaced out."

Dust in a Black Hole

Mrs. Arnold has something I call *with-it-ness*. If you wear new shoes to school, she spots them the moment you walk in. If you lose a tooth, she's already called the tooth fairy. New haircut? She'll tell you how much she loves it before your best friend does.

And if you are sitting slouchy in your seat, trying to look like you're paying attention when you're melting like butter from an *uh-oh* feeling, she's the first to know that something's wrong.

So while the rest of the kids in my class read books at their desks, Mrs. Arnold called me back to hers.

I looked at my toes and stood quietly. Mrs. Arnold patted my hand. "Tell me about it when you're ready."

I tilted my head toward the ceiling and thought.

Just that Monday, Mrs. Arnold created stars on that ceiling. In the real world, God made the stars.

God. He knew about my lie. And I knew about what was right. And wrong.

What had Dad said? Tell the truth even when it's hard to do.

But my lie trapped me like dust in a black hole. Telling the truth now would be harder than hard. It would be embarrassing.

It would be painful. I might get in trouble.

Let me tell you, pain is no fun.

Embarrassing isn't my favorite thing.

And I don't even want to talk about getting in trouble.

But . . . Dad also said the way we live matters to God.

That thought pulled like gravity on my heart, and BLAM! I realized it mattered to me too.

Closing my eyes, I bowed my head.

Hello, God. I want to do the right thing, but right now I'm afraid. I don't know where to start. Do you?

I opened my eyes. Mrs. Arnold was still there, studying my face.

My hands started sweating. I rubbed them against my pants. As seconds ticked away, my heart ticked with them. BUMP-

71

bump, BUMP-bump.

"Is this about space camp?" Mrs. Arnold asked in a soft voice.

I held my breath. How did Mrs. Arnold know?

"I'm asking because I looked up space camps online during lunch today," Mrs. Arnold said, as if she could read my mind. "I noticed they all have a minimum age requirement. Campers must be at least eight years old. And you're . . . ?"

My lip trembled. "Seven," I whispered. A tear leaked from my eye, and I wiped it away.

Mrs. Arnold raised an eyebrow. "I once told my best friend I had a pet horse," she said. "It wasn't true. When my friend asked to come see the horse, I made up excuse after excuse why she couldn't. We kept the horse in another state. We had loaned it to a neighbor. My lie was like a piece of gum stuck in my hair."

I cleared my throat. "Ryan got gum stuck in his hair once. When he tried to pull it out, it got stuck to his finger. And when he tried to pull it off that finger, it got stuck to another finger."

"Lies are like that," Mrs. Arnold said. "One thing leads to another, and before you know it, you're in a big gooey mess. Do you know what you have to do then?"

Because of what happened to Ryan's hair, I knew the answer.

And it's always good to know the answer when Mrs. Arnold asks a question.

"You cut it out," I said. "Even if it makes you look bad. And trust me, it usually does."

Mrs. Arnold looked thoughtful, like she was waiting for something.

"Oh," I said. "Oh. Yes. Well, about space camp . . . I . . . sort of . . . lied."

Even though I spoke in a tiny voice, I felt like my words rang out so loud that people in China could hear me.

Except I'm sure it didn't make any sense to them because they speak Chinese.

Still, I kept going. "I lied to you. And the class. And my friends. And to Sophie. I'm sorry! I didn't actually go to space camp."

"I know," Mrs. Arnold said. "I love you anyway."

"You do?" I said.

"And I'm proud that you finally told the truth."

I smiled a little. "You are?"

Nodding, she smiled a little back.

"But . . . how can I tell my friends?" I asked. "If I tell them, they'll be mad at me. If I don't, I'll have to keep lying more and more to cover up my first lie. And I think they'll probably find out anyway."

"That's a sticky, gooey problem," Mrs. Arnold agreed. "So . . . ?"

"So . . . maybe I should talk to Sophie from Mrs. Killeen's class? And Lynette too? And Kayla? And Ryan? And Adam?"

"I can arrange that," Mrs. Arnold said. She wrote a note and asked Lynette to carry it across the hall.

A few minutes later, Sophie came back with Lynette. Mrs. Arnold told us all to sit in the hallway and talk.

I felt the way an astronaut trapped in space with his oxygen running out would feel. Sick. Scared. And gaspy.

Meghan Rose Is
Out of This World

I sat in the hallway with Sophie, Lynette, Kayla, Ryan, and Adam. I must have looked terrible.

My friends looked confused.

Sophie looked glittery and sparkly. Well, she looked *angry,* glittery, and sparkly. All the bounce she had at recess was gone.

"This better be good," Sophie said. "I'm missing science. And I *like* science."

"It's . . . I want . . ." I took a big breath and spit out the truth. "I lied to everyone. I didn't go to space camp. I'm sorry."

Now one confused-looking face— Kayla's—and three more angry-looking faces stared back at me.

Sophie looked maddest of all. "Did you think going to space camp would steal my friend Carly away from me?"

"What? NO!"

Sophie crossed her arms. "I don't believe you. I only showed you my great jump roping and told you about the circus act so Carly would realize I was the best friend she could ever have. But you didn't like that, did you? I bet you came up with that whole space-camp thing to make me look bad in front of Carly."

"How could I make you look bad?" I

cried. "You are so WOWIE, and I'm just plain old me!"

"Then why did you do it?" Sophie demanded.

"I was afraid when my friends saw how well you jumped rope that you'd steal them away from me," I said. "I wanted to do something more exciting than you did. But I couldn't out-WOWIE you . . . so I lied."

"But you waved a long piece of grass around like a real space captain," Kayla said.

"I learned it from a TV show," I said.

"And the balloon rocket ship?" Adam asked.

"I figured out how a rocket works from a book."

Ryan snapped his fingers. "AHA!" he said. "So that's why you didn't laugh at my jokes. You were acting like a crazy spaceman."

"A what?" I said.

"An astro-NUT!" Ryan said. He high-fived Adam when I chuckled.

"Stop it, Ryan," Lynette said. "Meghan lied to us. That's not a joking matter!"

Everyone frowned.

"I'm sorry," I said.

"Don't ever do it again," Lynette said in a don't-even-think-about-messing-with-me kind of voice.

"Wait a minute!" Sophie said. "Meghan, did you say you think *I'm* WOWIE?"

"Yes," I said.

At first Sophie looked happy. Then the happy slid off her face. Her eyes flashed quick looks at everyone. "Um . . . I kind of lied too," she said in a tiny voice.

I nearly fell over. "What!"

"I went to dance camp," Sophie said, "but I wasn't the star in the high-wire act. One of the older girls got that part. I was in the regular group dance. I lied because I wanted to impress Carly. And . . . maybe you and your friends too."

We all sat in silence for a moment.

Then I said, "You know, even though you didn't get the starring role, I'm still impressed about the dance camp."

Sophie's blushed. "And even if you didn't go to space camp, I still love the balloon rocket."

I looked at the others. "So . . . will you forgive me?"

"Us," Sophie said.

Everyone nodded.

Good friends are like that. They forgive

you right when you need it most.

I turned to Sophie. "And . . . maybe we could start over."

"Maybe."

"Maybe you could play with my friends sometimes," I said. "I mean . . . *our* friends."

"*Our* friends?"

"Yes," I said. "I wanted to keep Lynette and Kayla and Adam and Ryan all to myself. But now I think that friends are for sharing, not owning or stealing or losing. Because everyone needs friends."

"Even friends who are crazy about ducks?" Kayla asked.

I nodded.

"Or friends who use big words like SESQUIPEDALIAN?" Lynette said.

"Or tell lame jokes?" Ryan said.

"Or . . . yo?" Adam said.

"Yes," I said. "And I think having friends you can always be honest with . . . friends you can always be yourself with no matter what . . . well, that's something out of this world!"

"Thank you," Sophie said.

My mouth dropped open. I'd never heard Sophie say thank-you before.

"Don't stare at me like that," Sophie snapped. Her old spunk was back. "Aren't you the one who's always saying it's polite to thank someone who's done something nice for you?"

I gave her a smile as big as Texas. "Now, that's the truth!"

1. Have you ever told a lie? Can you tell what happened and how you felt? If you were in that same situation again, would you do anything different? Why or why not? Read Psalm 34:13 and Psalm 15:1–2 for some good advice.

2. In the story, Meghan discovers two reasons why people lie. First, to impress others. Second, to avoid what will happen if they tell the truth. Can you think of any other reasons people might lie? Do you know who is never fooled by a lie? See Psalm 51:4 for the answer.

3. Bragging sometimes leads to lying. What are three things you can do to avoid that trap? Find out what the Bible says about this in Jeremiah 9:23–24.

4. Read John 4:23. (*The Message* has a good paraphrase of this passage.) What do you think it means to be honest from the inside out? What steps can you take each day to put this idea into practice?

5. Meghan apologized for lying and told the truth. How do you think the story would have been different if she hadn't done that? What do you think she'll do in the future if she's tempted to lie again? Why?

Blam! – Great Activity Ideas

1. Build a rocket or other space vehicle out of blocks, clay, or play dough. Or draw a picture. Write, show, or tell how the vehicle moves.

2. To gain some insight about the universe and outer space, read Isaiah 40:26, 45:12. Then use the Internet or a library book to find out all you can about our solar system. Create a model of the solar system. Some ideas: make a poster, use clay, paint Styrofoam balls, or use fruit to make an edible model. Be sure to label each planet.

3. Try Meghan's balloon-rocket experiment. It shows how fuel pushes a rocket forward. You will need a sturdy piece of string as

long as the room you will experiment in, a balloon, a straw, tape, and two helpers.

First, push the string through the straw. Keep the straw near one end and stretch the rest of the string across the room. One person will hold each end of the string. Keep the string *taut* (that means "tight"). A saggy string won't work!

Next, blow up the balloon but don't tie the end of it. Tape the balloon to the straw with the balloon opening facing the closest string holder. Count down and then let go of the balloon. It should fly across the room on the string.

4. Try an activity similar to the balloon-rocket experiment. You will need a balloon, a bendy straw, and a rubber band.

First, cut off two inches of the long part of the straw. Next, blow up the balloon but don't tie it off. While holding the air in the balloon, insert the long end of the straw into the balloon opening. Without letting out any air, twist a rubber band around the balloon opening to hold the straw in place.

Position the bendy part of the straw at an angle. Finally, let go of the balloon. It should spin around like a top! Based on the previous experiment, can you explain why that happens?

(Answer: the only way the air can get out of the balloon is through the straw. Since the straw is bent, the air turns on its way out . . . and so does the balloon!)

5. Make purple gravy for your mashed potatoes! You will need a package of white gravy mix, blue and red food coloring, and a handy adult.

First, follow the directions on the gravy mix package EXCEPT add three drops each of red and blue food coloring to the liquid part of the recipe. (Use more drops for a darker color.) Finish mixing as directed, serve, and eat. Yum!

6. Gravity pulls everything on planet Earth downward. Do you think it pulls heavy objects faster than light objects? To find out, try this gravity experiment. You will need a chair, aluminum foil, and one coin.

First, make two aluminum foil balls the same size. With one in each hand, stand on the chair. Hold your arms straight out from your body so that each ball is the same height from the floor. Let go of both balls at the same time. They should hit the floor at about the same time.

Now stand on the chair with arms held out with a foil ball in one hand and the coin in the other. Let go of both items at the same time. Do they hit the floor at the same time? Yes! That's because no matter what the weight of an object, gravity pulls everything downward at the same speed.

If you still don't believe it, try using other things around the house to see what happens. (Note: Some items, like paper and feathers, will have wind resistance. That may alter the outcome, so try to pick objects that won't have that problem.)

For Bob Wallace—LZS
For Katie and Kelsey—SC

Lori Z. Scott graduated from Wheaton College eons ago. She is a second-grade teacher, a wife, the mother of two busy teenagers, and a writer. Lori has published over one hundred articles, short stories, devotions, puzzles, and poems and has contributed to over a dozen books.

In her spare time Lori loves doodling, reading the Sunday comics, and making up lame jokes. You can find out more about Lori and her books at www.MeghanRoseSeries.com.

Stacy Curtis is a cartoonist, illustrator, printmaker, and twin who's illustrated over twenty children's books, including a *New York Times* best seller. He and his wife, Jann, live in Oak Lawn, Illinois, and happily share their home with their dog, Derby.